Hogs Back Books
The Stables
Down Place
Hogs Back
Guildford GU3 1DE
www.hogsbackbooks.com

Printed in China
ISBN: 978-1-907432-04-0
British Library Cataloguing-in-Publication Data.
A catalogue record for this book is available from the British Library.
1 3 5 4 2

For Nicole - KJH

For Siân - RG

With special thanks to Rachel and Lily.

Bella's Bubble

Karen Hodgson • Rebecca Griffiths

One day Granny gave Bella a bright red bottle.

"Thank you Granny," said Bella. "I love bubbles!"

"Let's see if you can blow a really big one!" said Granny.

Very gently Bella began to blow. And as she blew, a bubble grew ...

... and grew...

and grew...

and grew until ...

...it was **bigger** than Granny's prize pumpkin.

"Mummy, come and see!" called Bella, balancing the enormous bubble on the end of the wand.

"I'll be right there," said Mum.

But as she spoke, the wind blew and out of the window the bubble flew.

"My bubble!" cried Bella.

"Hurry, catch it!" said Granny.

Quick as a flash, Bella ran down the hall and out of the door.

In the garden Pebbles was chasing butterflies.

The bubble drifted gently towards the kitten.

Pebbles lifted up a sharp claw.

"No!" cried Bella.

But then the wind blew and off the bubble flew.

(Phew!)

Higher and higher it went, wobbling along the path

towards Bertie, who was busy playing pirates.

"Shiver me timbers!" shouted Bertie
when he saw the gigantic bubble. He
reached towards it brandishing his wooden
sword.

"No!" cried Bella.

But then the wind blew and
off the bubble flew.

(Phew!)

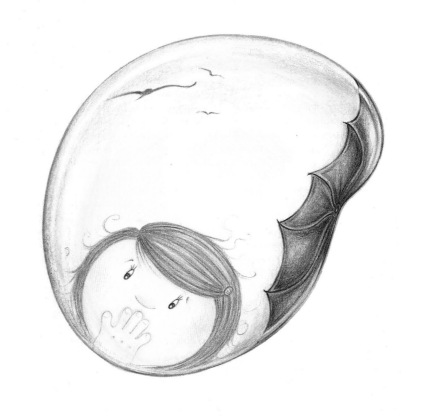

Higher and higher it went, down the street towards

Mr Poppit, who was striding along twirling and whirling his umbrella.

Its sharp tip turned towards the bubble.

"No!" cried Bella.

But then the wind blew and
off the bubble flew.

(Phew!)

Higher and higher it went, over the fence and into the park, where the holly trees swayed in the breeze. Their prickly leaves bent towards the bubble.

"No!" cried Bella.

But then the wind blew and
off the bubble flew.

(Phew!)

Higher and higher it went, into the churchyard.

The church steeple shone in the sun and on top an old brass weather vane swung around and around. Its rusty arrow pointed straight at the bubble.

"No!" cried Bella.

But then the wind blew and
off the bubble flew.

(Phew!)

Higher and higher it climbed, over the fields.

In the distance Bella saw a dazzling rainbow.

"Oh!" she gasped.

BOIN G G!

The bubble bounced off the rainbow. It shot past the
church steeple, shining in the sun ...

... past the holly trees, swaying in the breeze ...

... past Mr Poppit's twirling, whirling umbrella ...

... past Bertie the Pirate's wooden sword ...

... past Pebbles' sharp claws ...

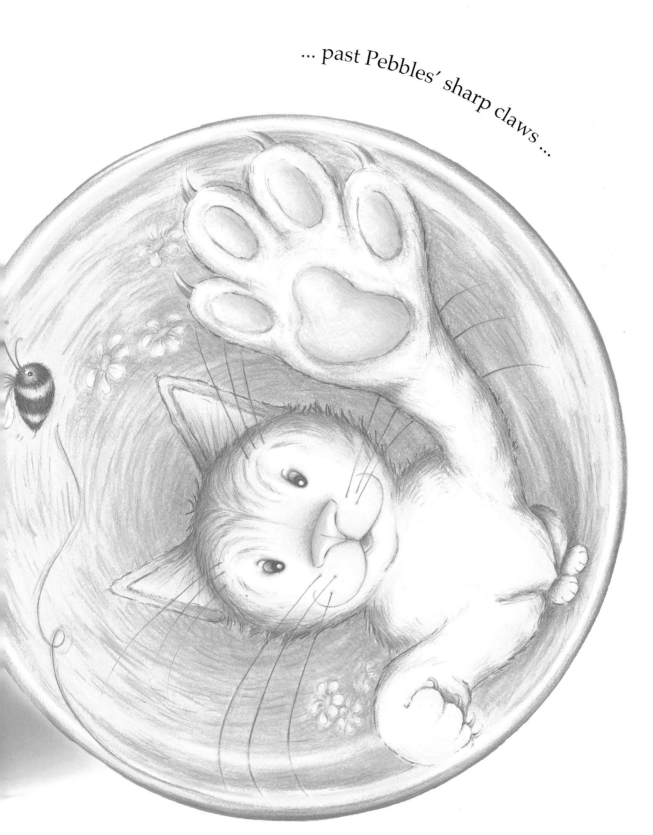

... back through the window and into
the house, where it landed with an
enormous ...

...pop!

... on Granny's pointy nose.

"I saw it!" said Mum.

The
End